For Sielle

First published in the United States of America in 2014 by
Chronicle Books LLC.

First published in France in 2012 under the title *Coquillages
et petit ours* by hélium, 18, rue Séguier 75006 Paris.

Library of Congress Cataloging-in-Publication Data available.

ISBN 978-1-4521-2743-9

Manufactured in China.

MIX
Paper from
responsible sources
FSC® C104723

Typeset in ClickClack.

10 9 8 7 6 5 4 3 2 1

Chronicle Books LLC
680 Second Street, San Francisco, California 94107

Chronicle Books—we see things differently. Become part
of our community at www.chroniclekids.com.

the
BEAR'S
SEA
ESCAPE

BENJAMIN CHAUD

chronicle books·san francisco

igh atop the opera house with snowflakes falling fast, Papa Bear and his cub snuffle their snouts up through the snow. "We can't stay here!" Papa Bear grumbles. "This is no place for a nice long nap."

Up and then down, climbing over chimneys and racing across rafters,
Papa Bear and Little Bear slide over the city's snow-covered slopes in
search of a warm place to sleep.

Look at all the bears dozing in this cozy den! Papa Bear and Little Bear agree that this must be the perfect place to hibernate, so they cuddle in close to start snoozing the winter away.

But while the sleepy bears slumber, a little boy finds a new furry friend in Little Bear, and quickly adopts him as his own! Papa Bear is just too deep in drowsy dreams to notice his Little Bear leaving!

When Papa Bear discovers that his cub has departed, he borrows a scooter and sets off on his search.

As Papa Bear whizzes through the busy city streets, he wonders, "Oh, where could my Little Bear be?"

Meanwhile, the little boy, now at a train station across town, is surprised to learn that his new toy bear is more *bear* and less *toy*!

With a huff and a puff, Papa Bear reaches the station just as Little
Bear hops on board. With no time to lose, Papa Bear clings tightly to the
caboose and tries to imagine where the train tracks might lead them. . . .

To the port, of course! The train has reached the sea. Everyone is scrambling and scampering onto the ship, ready for their sea adventure to begin!

With a little help, Papa Bear manages to board the big ocean liner, and he spots his cute cub below. But Little Bear is too busy taking in the fresh salty air to notice his high-flying papa.

Poor Papa Bear! He is terribly lost on the big cruise ship, and his cub is nowhere to be seen!

Just where could that Little Bear be hiding now?

Perhaps Little Bear went for a swim? Papa Bear dives into the sea to explore for himself.

"Have you seen my Little Bear?" he asks a puzzled puffer fish. The reef is brimming with bubbles and barnacles, scales and seaweed, but there is no sign of fluffy brown bear fur for as far as the eye can see!

Once on shore, Papa Bear is certain that he will find his cub. But there is just too much hustle and hubbub on the beach to find a hairy Little Bear.

With sand between his toes, and flowers stuck to his fur, Papa Bear spies a jungle ahead. Could Little Bear be nestled among the trees?

What a maze of stairs and leaves, with wild animals everywhere!
Surprises lurk behind every leaf. Could Little Bear be hiding here?

Up and around the winding path, Papa Bear follows the sound of music and the stamping of feet until . . .

. . . he is swept up into a dance! Out of the island's jungle and back on the beach, a conga line snakes its way through the crowd. Papa Bear searches for his Little Bear, trying not to step on any toes!

Now, really! Where could Little Bear be amid this masquerade madness?

From atop the dinner table, Little Bear trumpets his own tune, a song that he knows his Papa Bear will love.

ooooooooaaaaaap !

"There is my Little Bear!" Papa Bear exclaims, still dancing to the rhythm of Little Bear's beat. "Let's take a break from our boogying and enjoy this feast!"

Beneath the swaying palms and beside the beach bonfire, Papa Bear settles in to sleep among the fragrant island flowers. "Little Bear, aren't you going to go to sleep, too?"

"Just one more song!" Little Bear pleads. "I wrote this lullaby just for you, about a Little Bear and his Papa Bear, hibernating by the sea, where the sun will keep them warm and fill their winter dreams."

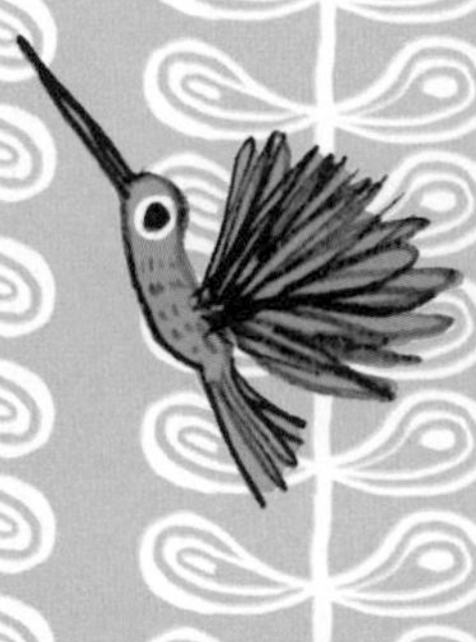